15.95

BRENDA SHANNON YEE

Hide & Seek

illustrated by DEBBIE TILLEY

Orchard Books • New York

An Imprint of Scholastic Inc.

Orchard Books
An Imprint of Scholastic Inc.
95 Madison Avenue, New York, NY 10016

Manufactured in the United States of America
Printed and bound by Phoenix Color Corp.
Book design by Nancy Goldenberg
The text of this book is set in 54 point Lemonade .
The illustrations are pen and ink and watercolor.

1 3 5 7 9 10 8 6 4 2

Library of Congress Cataloging-in-Publication Data
Yee, Brenda Shannon.
Hide & seek / by Brenda Shannon Yee ; illustrated by Debbie Tilley.
p. cm.
Summary: A mouse plays hide-and-seek with the owner of a house.
ISBN 0-531-30302-0 (trade : alk paper)
[1. Mice–Fiction. 2. Hide-and-seek–Fiction. 3. Stories in rhyme.]
I. Tilley, Debbie, ill. II. Title.
PZ8.3.Y4 Hi 2001 [E]–dc21 99-87008

For Carolyn and Caity
—B.S.Y.

For my daughter,
Gillian Elizabeth Will (BUG),
born 12-8-99
Love, Mom
—D.T.

I hide.

You seek.

I call,

"Don't peek!"

"1, 2."

Tiptoe shoe.

"3, 4."

Creep to door.

"5, 6."

Old door sticks.

"7, 8."

Spy a crate.

"9, 10."

Quick! Dive in!

"Ready or not!

Here I come!"

I hear,

creak, creak.

You

leap!

I

shriek!

"Let's play

again!"

"You hide.

I seek."